NICKELODEON

h2o
Just add water!

Fishy Business

Read other titles in the series

NICKELODEON

h2o
Just add water!

Fishy Business

Adapted by Rachel Elliot

SIMON AND SCHUSTER

SIMON AND SCHUSTER
First published in Great Britain in 2009 by Simon & Schuster UK Ltd,
1st Floor, 222 Gray's Inn Road, London WC1X 8HB
A CBS Company
Originally published in Australia in 2007 by Parragon
Licenced by ZDF Enterprises GmbH, Mainz

A CIP catalogue record for this book is available from the British Library

ISBN 978-1-84738-539-0

10 9 8 7 6 5 4 3 2 1

Printed by CPI Cox & Wyman, Reading, Berkshire RG1 8EX

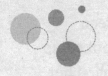

Chapter 1

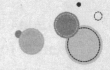

It was evening on the Gold Coast and the sun had set. The lights from the waterside houses were shining out over the canal. The moon was reflected in the dark, rippling water. A single boat cruised slowly past Cleo Sertori's house, where lights were gleaming in the front windows. Ominous sounds were echoing through the dark from Cleo's house – pulsing, threatening sounds.

Cleo's parents and her sister, Kim, were sitting in the lounge room, their eyes glued to the TV screen. They were watching a documentary about the eating habits of great white sharks.

"Nasty," said Cleo's dad, Don, shaking the remote at the TV. "You don't want to mess with one of those."

His feet were resting on the coffee table and

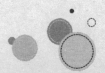

he didn't even jump as the shark on screen went in for the kill. Cleo's mum, Bev, looked up from the plate she was polishing and rolled her eyes. She wasn't particularly interested in these documentaries about the deep, but her husband had been a commercial fisherman all his working life, and he was fascinated by anything to do with the sea.

"Have you ever seen a great white, Dad?" asked Kim, who was feeling very tense, but completely fascinated.

"Only once," said Don, in a dark, serious tone, remembering the long-ago day. "Took half my catch for the day and then they shredded my net."

He cast his mind back. Don was no coward, but that attack on his boat had made his blood run cold.

"You don't mess with 'em," he said. "They'll rip ya to bits. Tiny bits. Little, teeny weeny bits."

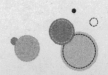

Don held his fingers apart by a very small amount to show just how tiny the bits would be. Kim was spooked, and so was Cleo. She was standing in the doorway to the kitchen, holding a dishcloth and staring at the TV screen.

Why would anyone want to watch that kind of thing? she thought. *It's horrible ... and scary ... and I can't even look!*

She took a few steps forward and looked at the sofa where her family was curled up.

"Kim?" she said meaningfully, glaring at her little sister.

Kim ignored her. Her eyes were riveted to the screen.

"*Kim!*" hissed Cleo, jerking her head towards the kitchen.

Kim stood up reluctantly and followed Cleo into the kitchen. Cleo turned and held out the dishcloth.

"Ah, dishes?" she demanded, glaring accusingly.

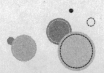

It was a couple of weeks since Cleo and her two best friends, Rikki Chadwick and Emma Gilbert, had been stuck in a drifting boat on the open sea. They had landed on Mako Island and discovered a secret cave, where something magical had happened to them. Ever since that night, their lives had changed completely. Now, they only had to touch a drop of water and within ten seconds they turned into real-life mermaids, complete with tails and scales. Rikki and Emma seemed to be having fun with it, but for Cleo it was nothing but a nightmare. It was even cleaning her out of pocket money. There was no way she could risk doing the washing up any more, but washing up was one of her chores, and there was only one way to persuade her sister to do it for her …

"Ten dollars," said Kim.

"*What?*" Cleo whispered. "You only charged five to do them yesterday!"

"You want me to keep doing your chores?" Kim enquired with an angelic smile. "Well, my

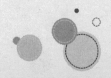

price has gone up. Besides, I want to watch TV. Ten dollars."

Cleo folded her arms and scowled. *This is daylight robbery!* she thought. *I can't believe my own sister is so mean!*

"No way," she declared.

"What's up with you, anyway?" asked Kim, screwing up her face in deep thought. "I know you're scared of water but this is ridiculous."

Kim waited curiously for an answer, and Cleo felt a shock of adrenalin race through her body. She was sure that it was only a matter of time before someone worked out what was going on. *It's so obvious that I have a problem with water*, she thought. *How am I ever going to keep this secret from my own family?*

Rikki and Emma had made Cleo promise not to tell another soul. If anyone found out, they were convinced that all three of them would be taken away and treated like science experiments. The only other person who knew

the truth was Cleo's friend Lewis, and he was fascinated by it because he loved the mysteries of science. But Cleo knew that there was no way that Kim or her parents would understand!

"Fine, ten," Cleo snapped, shoving the cloth into Kim's hand before she asked any more awkward questions. "I'll pay you later."

Cleo marched back into the lounge room, where her dad was still watching the TV.

"Cleo, check this out!" he said with enthusiasm. "This is the best part – it's the feeding frenzy."

Chomping sounds came from the television and Cleo watched, feeling slightly sick. Seeing creatures with tails being eaten suddenly had a whole new meaning for her. She felt strangely dizzy, and then angry with her dad. *Why does he think that this is entertainment?* she thought. *It's horrible – it's like a real-life horror film.* Cleo had never liked anything gruesome, but now it made her flesh creep.

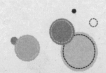

"How can you even *watch* this stuff?" she demanded.

She rushed out of the room and ran upstairs. Her parents watched her go and then looked at each other, surprised. Cleo was usually very easy-going and happy, but recently they had noticed a definite change in her mood. Bev had put it down to Cleo being a teenager, but Don knew better … something was definitely wrong.

Don frowned. He and his eldest daughter had always been close, but just recently she had seemed somehow distant and unapproachable. Things had been really busy at work – his partner had been off sick – and his mind had been taken up with that. *I guess I haven't been paying attention to Cleo like I should have done*, he thought. *As soon as Gus is back at work, I'll take a couple of days off and we'll spend some quality time together.*

Happy now that he had mentally solved the problem already, Don settled back and carried on watching the feeding frenzy.

Upstairs, Cleo shut her door and flung herself on her bed. Silently, she lay face down, wishing that she could turn back the clock. If only she hadn't ended up on Mako Island that day, they would never have found the magical cave and none of this would have happened.

I'm a mer-freak now, she thought, and tears pricked her eyes. *No one understands. Emma and Rikki think that being a mermaid is the best thing that's ever happened to them. Lewis just goes on about the amazing scientific side of it. No one seems to be having the problems I'm having with it!*

Cleo thumped her pillow and sat up, staring straight ahead with unseeing eyes. *Sooner or later, I'm going to lose it completely*, she thought, miserably. *I just don't know how much more of this I can take.*

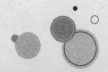

Chapter 2

Early the next morning, the sun was shining and the sea was warm and inviting. A surfer raced down the beach and launched himself into the water on his board, paddling out to sea with his arms. A few metres ahead of him, a girl was waiting for the perfect wave, belly down on her surfboard. Even further out and far below the surface, where the reef began and the sun was sparkling on the turquoise water, two mermaids were playing with a school of fish.

Rikki and Emma chased the fish through the tropical reef, creating a rush of bubbles amid the vivid colours and serene beauty of the tropical reef. *It's a wonderland*, Emma thought as she curved around a bright orange fish with a tail like a fan. *It's like the best dream I've ever had – and it just keeps getting better!* She exchanged a happy smile with Rikki, who was

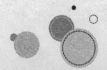

alight with excitement. They swam shoulder to shoulder, staying in rhythm with each other as they undulated through the water. After trying many different techniques, they had found that the fastest way to swim was with their arms stretched out in front of them and their hands slightly arched … although when she got excited Rikki always forgot about this and just waved her arms about in delight! Once, this would have annoyed Emma, but now she knew Rikki better. She realized that Rikki was driven by passion and that she found a sort of blazing joy in this new underwater world.

Although they couldn't speak underwater, swimming alongside each other had made them like and understand each other much better than words ever could. They were linked by the their secret, and by their love of the ocean.

Rikki glanced at Emma, who was smiling as she swam gracefully over a huge expanse of living coral. *Emma's so honest*, she thought. *She would never let her friends down. I've never met*

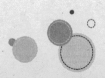

anyone quite like her before!

They had already spent an hour testing their abilities, playing and timing themselves as they swam. They dived down to see another school of fish, and then timed themselves in another race. Each swim they had allowed them to learn more about being mermaids, and to use their skills and powers better and better. They paused for a while, half hiding behind a rock to watch some of the shyer fish swim by. Their blonde hair floated in the water like liquid gold.

Finally Emma tapped her wrist and jerked her head. They were going to be late for school if they didn't hurry, and Emma wanted to go to the Juice-Net Café before her first lesson. She hadn't been able to reach Cleo on the phone that morning, and she had been hoping to persuade her to come for a swim. *I wish I knew how to help her,* Emma thought. *Cleo has been so touchy lately. I hate seeing her like that.*

With one last flick of their tails, they turned

and rocketed through the water back towards the shore.

Emma and Rikki strolled into the Juice-Net Café and ordered some smoothies, chattering excitedly about their swim and what they had discovered about their abilities. They grabbed a table and sipped their drinks, going over the things they had seen and done, and talking about the sensation of swimming with a tail. Then Emma looked up and saw Lewis coming towards them with a fruit juice in his hand. Emma beamed at him and started speaking before he even had a chance to sit down.

"You won't believe it," she declared. "We've timed ourselves – and guess how long we can hold our breath for?"

"Umm ..." said Lewis, making some calculations in his head.

Emma realized that Lewis was the wrong person to ask something like that – he was actually trying to scientifically work out the answer before she told him!

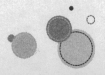

"Fifteen minutes!" she said in triumph.

Rikki held up her palm and Emma high-fived it – they made quite a team!

"Impressive," said Lewis, taking a seat.

"Yep!" said Rikki with a wide smile. "It's pretty cool."

"I bet we can stay down for longer if we really try," Emma continued.

"You're on," said Rikki, rising to the challenge with a sparkle in her eyes.

"You think you can beat me?" said Emma, turning to Rikki and grinning.

"I *know* I can," Rikki laughed, playing along with Emma's good mood. "Bring it on."

"You girls must be jumping out of your skin about this stuff!" said Lewis, smiling at the girls' banter.

"Yeah!" said Emma.

Rikki nodded, her blue eyes aglow.

"Well," added Emma meaningfully, "*two* of

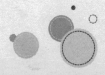

us are …"

Just then Cleo walked into the café and made her way towards them. Lewis spotted her and his face broke into a smile.

"Hey, Cleo, guess what?" he called, pointing at Emma and Rikki. "These guys can hold their breath for 15 minutes!"

Emma and Rikki glared at him.

"Lewis!" they cried in unison.

"Sorry," he said quickly, realizing that they could be overheard.

Cleo sat down and looked at them with a very serious expression on her face.

"What's going on?" she enquired.

"We've been – you know... *swimming*," said Emma.

A sort of blank, frozen look passed over Cleo's face. She nodded, but her eyes dropped and the corners of her mouth turned down slightly.

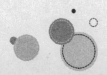

"It's the best thing," said Rikki eagerly. "The reef is out of this world."

Cleo widened her eyes and forced a smile, which appeared so briefly that Rikki almost thought she had imagined it.

"That's great," Cleo said, clearly uninterested. "So has anyone been able to finish that calculus homework?"

Lewis nodded proudly, his eyes fixed on Cleo's face.

Rikki's shoulders slumped. *Why does Cleo have to be so defensive about this?* she wondered. *If only she'd try it, I'm sure she'd love it!*

"Question seven's a nightmare," Cleo went on.

"We missed you this morning," said Emma, leaning forward across the table. "Why weren't you answering your phone?"

When Emma had phoned, Cleo had been in the bathroom, looking at her enormous tail as it hung over the edge of the bath. Rikki and

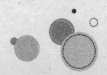

Emma were able to think of it as a wonderful sight, but to her it was freakish and repulsive. She carried on as if Emma hadn't even spoken.

"And that project on geography – that's due on Thursday," she said, her eyes flicking nervously from side to side. "We really need to get together on that one."

Lewis was listening intently, but Rikki and Emma exchanged glances. Rikki was growing very weary of Cleo's fears, but Emma was desperate to make her see that the water was nothing to be afraid of. She took a deep breath.

"Cleo, listen," said Rikki in a tired, patient voice. "Whatever has happened to us is incredible. You've *got* to come out with us – the water is amazing."

Cleo's face fell and she rolled her eyes. *Why can't they just shut up about the water?* she thought furiously. *I'm sick of hearing about it!*

"I'm not doing it, okay?" she snapped. "I didn't ask for any of this to happen to us, so stop bugging me about it."

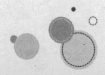

She gazed at each of them for a moment. No one said a word. Lewis rubbed his neck nervously. Cleo stood up and walked off to school alone. *That told them*, she thought. *Now they had just better leave me alone – I never want to hear the words 'beach' or 'sea' ever again!*

Rikki glanced at Emma, who just raised her eyebrows. They hated arguing with Cleo, but neither of them had the faintest idea how to persuade her that being in the water was the most wonderful feeling in the world.

Lewis cleared his throat. *This is up to me*, he thought. *Cleo's had a problem with swimming ever since she was little. But I know how she ticks; I'm sure that I can bring her round.*

He told Rikki and Emma to leave it to him. He would find the right words and persuade Cleo to get into the water.

But Emma and Rikki just looked at one another as Lewis waved at them and headed off to school. They weren't holding out much hope.

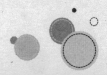

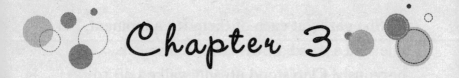

Chapter 3

The school was bustling with students on their way to their first lessons. Kids were riding up on bikes and strolling in on foot from all directions. Friends called out to each other and walked arm in arm, gossiping. At one end of the central quadrangle, Miriam, the golden girl of the school, was busy flirting with Zane Bennett. Teachers hurried past with armfuls of homework and students gathered around their lockers and their classroom doors, trying to put off the moment when they would have to go inside and start working.

Cleo walked into the quadrangle alone, feeling angry and tearful. She usually walked to school with Rikki and Emma, and it felt weird and lonely to be by herself. She was determined not to cry, but all she really felt like doing was running home and hiding in her bedroom.

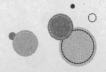

Everyone's happy apart from me, she thought, gazing around at her fellow students. It seemed as if they were all laughing and joking, just to make her feel worse. Cleo felt as though she was cut off from everyone, trapped in some sort of bubble. It was as if she was cut off from everyone she had ever trusted, and she didn't know what to do.

I guess I'll just have to get used to it, she decided. *Rikki and Emma are always going to be off together, messing around in the water. Why can't they understand that just being on the beach is scary for me, let alone actually getting into the water!*

Cleo thought about the shark documentary her dad had been watching the night before and shivered sadly. *I can't talk to anyone*, she realized. *I can't tell anyone about being a ... a mermaid, and I can't talk to Rikki or Emma about how scary it is, because that's not how they feel. I can't even talk to Lewis.*

Just then, Byron, the school's surfing champ,

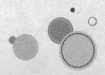

walked up behind her.

"Hey, Cleo," he called out in his usual laid-back style.

Cleo stopped in her tracks. Even though she was lonely, she really didn't feel like talking to anyone either.

"You've got to come down the beach," Byron said, stopping next to her with his satchel slung casually over his shoulder.

Cleo spun around, resentment suddenly sweeping through her like fire.

"*Why?*" she yelled. "Why does *everyone* want me to come down the beach?"

She stomped off and Byron jogged after her.

"Hey, chill, all right?" he said in alarm.

Cleo stopped again and looked at his worried face. She felt a rush of guilt and her shoulders slumped.

"Sorry … I'm a bit tense," she said, trying to make amends. "What's going on?"

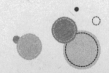

"I saw the first of this season's turtles laying eggs this morning at the beach," said Byron, a huge smile spreading over his face. "It was amazing."

"Wow," said Cleo, feeling glad that Byron hadn't taken offence. "That's wonderful."

"Yeah," Byron agreed, his face falling, "but I heard a rumour that one of them got caught in a fishing net heading back out to sea."

"Oh!" said Cleo, horrified. "Poor little thing."

They walked along together towards the lockers. Cleo forgot about her troubles for a moment and thought about the turtles instead. They were an endangered species, but even though they had troubles, they just kept coming back to the beaches and laying more eggs. *They're so inspiring*, Cleo thought. *I wish that I could do something to protect them. What kind of mean fisherman would allow a sea turtle to drown in his nets?*

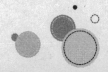

Cleo stopped next to her locker. Byron kept walking and waved at her as he went.

"See you," he said, heading off to his first class of the day.

Cleo waved back as he strolled away. *Byron's such a cool guy*, she thought, *He's always so chilled out and happy.*

She opened her locker and took out her atlas for her geography class. She was starting to feel a little bit better. Just because Emma and Rikki couldn't talk about anything except their swimming abilities, that didn't mean that she didn't have other friends to hang out with and other things to think about. *I'll just think about those poor sea turtles*, she told herself. *I'll try to think of some way to help them out.*

A little further down the hallway, Lewis was watching her carefully. He gave a little smile as Byron strolled past him, and then walked towards Cleo, who was still pulling her books out of her locker.

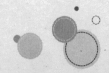

"Hey Cleo," he said, trying to think of something 'normal' to say. "Do you want to go and hang out at the mall later?"

Cleo looked up at him and his heart plummeted as a frozen, blank look came over her face.

"I'm busy, sorry," she said, closing her locker door.

Lewis closed his eyes for a moment. He knew Cleo's moods of old. *She's got to face up to this*, he thought. *I don't want to be in the middle of her and Rikki and Emma!* He tried another tack.

"Cleo, look," he said softly. "I know these … recent developments … have hit you pretty hard, but you can't hide forever."

Cleo leaned back against the lockers, not meeting his eyes. *Why does he have to bring this up now?* she thought. *I can't think about that. I'm thinking about cute little sea turtles and all those eggs they're laying on the beach …*

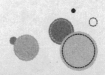

"Just because you're a ... a mermaid – " he went on.

Lewis hadn't realized quite how sensitive Cleo was feeling. Her temper flared up again and she forgot all about the sea turtles. The very word 'mermaid' made her skin crawl. It made her think about that shark documentary, and about drowning and danger.

"I am not one of those ... *things*!" she declared, turning to him and stopping him mid-sentence. "I've *never* liked the water. And I never *will*."

She held his gaze for a moment as he stared at her in astonishment. Then she pushed past him and walked away swiftly.

"What are you going to do – hide from water for the rest of your life?" Lewis called after her, thoroughly exasperated.

She turned and paused. For a moment Lewis thought that she was going to walk back to him. But she just frowned and lowered her eyes, as if

to say 'If I have to.' Then she turned and carried on walking.

Lewis felt a lump in his throat. She had gone, leaving him concerned and confused. He had never had trouble getting through to Cleo before. Was she going to shut down completely? What if this was the end of their friendship? *I can't handle that*, Lewis thought. *I can't lose Cleo. I've got to do something!*

The day had started badly and it just got worse. Cleo went out of her way to avoid Lewis, Emma and Rikki. At lunchtime they couldn't find her anywhere, and in the classes they shared she sat as far away from them as possible and kept her head down. Rikki, who always liked to take the bull by the horns, wanted to confront her. Even Emma suggested that they sit down with Cleo and talk the whole thing through, once and for all. But Lewis convinced them to give him some more time. He was sure that he would find a way to get

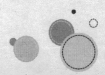

through to Cleo, and he didn't want Rikki to go wading in and upsetting her. *Rikki's nice*, he thought. *But she can be really, really scary sometimes, and right now, Cleo just needs a bit of space.*

By the end of the day, Emma and Rikki were feeling very frustrated. They had their last class together – chemistry – and they spent so much time in the lesson whispering that their teacher had to tell them both off. Rikki was used to getting told off, of course – that was pretty much a daily occurrence. But for Emma it was a new experience. Under normal circumstances, she would have been completely mortified. But nothing was normal any more. Right now, all Emma cared about was making sure that Cleo was okay.

Chapter 4

The after-school bell sounded and students poured out of their classrooms. As Rikki and Emma left the chemistry lab, Lewis walked up to them, looking dejected. It had been a long, difficult day. Every time he had tried to talk to Cleo, she had just cut him dead or walked away. He had said and done everything he could think of, and he didn't know what else to try.

The girls saw the expression on his face and guessed what it meant. The three of them stood in the hallway and stared at each other.

"You bombed out, right?" said Rikki in her usual blunt way.

Lewis bridled for a moment and started to defend himself.

"She's just taking a little time to …" he began, and then he paused, realizing that it was

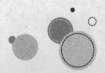

time to admit defeat. "Yeah, I bombed out."

He shrugged as Rikki and Emma sighed. Just then, Cleo came down the steps towards them. Rikki and Emma looked up at her, and Lewis guessed what they were thinking.

"Er, I am pretty sure she doesn't want to talk about it," he warned them quickly.

Cleo had paused halfway down the steps and was staring at them. She hesitated, her hand on the railing. If she walked down there they were bound to say something about the mermaid thing. But if she turned around and went back the way she had come, it would be obvious that she didn't want to talk to them. Cleo sighed. *The thing is, I really do want to talk to them!* she thought. *I really miss them. I've wanted to talk to them all day. Just not about mermaids!*

Emma looked up at Cleo and then back at Lewis again. *If you want something done properly, don't ask a boy*, she thought. *Some things need a girl's touch.*

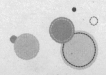

"Forget it, Lewis," she said, slapping him on the back. "We can deal with this. It's a girl thing."

Rikki nodded approvingly and Lewis winced as she and Emma walked up to Cleo. He knew that Emma would try to say the right thing, but Rikki could be a little … impatient. Sometimes – just *sometimes* – she opened her mouth without thinking. He gulped and crossed his fingers for good luck.

Cleo saw them coming and turned her back on them, leaning on the railing and staring out over the quadrangle.

Lewis watched anxiously as the girls walked up behind her. She was trying to look relaxed, but he could see that her arms were twitching and her shoulders were tense. Cleo hated confrontation, and now it seemed as if there was no way out of it.

She turned to look at Emma and Rikki.

"Cleo," Emma began. "About this whole mermaid business ..."

Cleo looked at her coldly. Emma paused, uncertain how to continue. *I've never seen Cleo look like that before*, she thought.

Cleo was weighing up her choices. She knew that she had to have this conversation with Emma and Rikki, but she really wasn't looking forward to it. After a moment she decided that she should just take a leaf out of Rikki's book and say exactly what was on her mind.

"There are more important things in life than seeing how long you can hold your breath and frolicking with the dolphins you know," she said firmly, waving her arm vaguely in Rikki's direction.

"I don't *frolic*," said Rikki, opening her eyes wide at this slur. "I *glide*."

Cleo twisted her fingers together as Rikki's blue gaze burned into hers. Rikki certainly knew how to deliver a killer look, but right now Cleo was too upset to let it affect her.

"Whatever," she said, her dark eyebrows

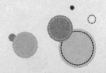

slanting in a deep frown. "It's not important. I don't want to talk about it."

Emma could hardly believe her ears. There were other students milling around and she was conscious that she couldn't speak too loudly, but she had to make her point.

"How can you say that?" she asked, as Cleo rolled her eyes. "This is the most amazing thing that's ever happened to us. Probably the most amazing thing that's ever happened to anybody!"

Rikki stared unblinkingly at Cleo. *Emma's right*, she thought. *This is huge! It's life changing! How can Cleo not be interested in something this awesome? And how can she think that I frolic?*

Emma flicked a strand of hair out of her eyes and waited. She felt a bit as if they were bullying Cleo, who was obviously on the defensive. But this thing was happening to them whether they liked it or not, and she couldn't bear to see her best friend so unhappy.

Cleo looked up at the sky, wishing that it would open up and take her away from this horrible conversation. She cast her mind around for something – *anything* – that would change the subject.

"Well, what about the turtles?" she demanded.

Rikki frowned at Emma, who shrugged.

"Turtles?" she asked.

"Apparently a sea turtle got caught in a fishing net this morning," Cleo told them. "*That's* important."

She spat out the words at Rikki, hoping to make her think about something else. But to her amazement, Rikki didn't turn a hair.

"I don't believe this," said Rikki, with a mirthless smile. "You're such a hypocrite."

"Why?" said Cleo, startled. She had been expecting Rikki to drag the conversation back to talking about mermaids – not to start accusing her of hypocrisy.

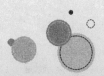

"Cleo, your dad's a fisherman," said Rikki impatiently, annoyed that she had been drawn into this conversation. "His nets are the ones trapping the turtles."

"That's not true," said Cleo simply. "My dad would never do that."

"Really?" said Rikki, levelling her clear, questioning gaze at Cleo.

The two girls stared at each other coldly, neither one prepared to back down. *She's so arrogant!* Cleo thought, narrowing her eyes. *My dad would never hurt those turtles ... would he?*

A whisper of doubt niggled at the back of her mind. She pushed past Rikki and walked away, feeling angry and worried.

Rikki turned to Emma and shrugged as Lewis came to join them. Cleo's constant fears and doubts were annoying sometimes, but what really got on her nerves was people refusing to face the cold, hard truth. *It's about time that Cleo accepted the truth*, she thought. *She's a*

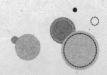

mermaid, and no amount of whining about fishermen and sea turtles is going to change that.

Now that the girls had bombed out too, Lewis felt a little better. He just hoped that sooner or later, Cleo would come round and be happy to talk about the whole mermaid thing. *It would be so cool to be able to hear Cleo talking about holding her breath for fifteen minutes or swimming with dolphins,* he thought. *I wish that there was some way to help her like the water.*

Emma was staring after Cleo's retreating back with a concerned frown on her face. She knew how close Cleo was to her dad, but she also knew that Rikki was right. If the local fishermen were using illegal nets, they had to be stopped, or more poor turtles could be killed.

Lost in their own thoughts, Rikki, Emma and Lewis headed across the quadrangle and out of school. Somehow, they had to find a way to make Cleo accept who … and *what* … she now was.

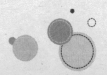

Chapter 5

Cleo hurried home through the park, feeling shaken and hurt. She couldn't stop thinking about the turtles – or about what Rikki had said. Was it possible that her dad was helping to endanger a whole species? She couldn't believe it – she *wouldn't* believe it! But there was a doubting voice right in the back of her mind, asking *are you sure*?

She walked swiftly, her legs feeling wobbly underneath her. The people that she passed seemed to be looking at her strangely, and she felt as if she was going to burst into tears. She walked faster and faster as she grew closer to her home, until by the time she reached her driveway she was running up it. She flung open the door, dashed inside and slammed it behind her, leaning against it and shaking.

This is ridiculous, she told herself. *Rikki*

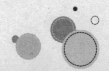

doesn't know my dad – he would never do this! I'm not going to waste another thought on her stupid accusations!

She went up to her room and opened her school bag. Homework might not be much fun, but it was a sure-fire way to take her mind off Rikki Chadwick and her silly ideas.

Cleo tried to do her calculus homework, but the numbers seemed to be dancing all over the page, and she couldn't focus for two minutes together. She threw down her pen and picked up a textbook, but that was no good either. Images of sea turtles, sharks and mermaids kept swimming through her mind.

Cleo stood up and paced up and down her room, staring moodily at her fish tank. It was no use pretending – the thought that her dad might be harming sea turtles was awful, and she couldn't dismiss it from her mind. Her fears and concerns about being a mermaid were brushed aside by a sweeping, overwhelming sense of dread and shame. *Rikki thinks that Dad is*

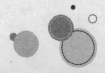

catching those turtles, she thought, torturing herself. *Emma must think so too – she didn't argue when Rikki said it. Maybe everyone thinks so! Maybe that's why Byron came and told me about the sea turtle that got caught. What if he thinks that Dad had something to do with it?*

Cleo's face darkened as she frowned and clenched her fists. *It's not true!* she told herself. *I don't believe it! Dad wouldn't do that!* She sat down at her desk and picked up her textbook again. But she just kept reading the same sentence over and over, until the words on the page spiralled and blurred, and tears splashed down onto the page. Just at that moment, her mum called her for dinner. Cleo slammed the textbook shut, angrily swept the tears off her cheeks and then made her way downstairs.

Cleo was completely silent throughout dinner. She felt as if her mind was on a loop, going over and over the same arguments and thoughts until she wanted to scream. While her dad told a few jokes and her mum told them about the latest neighbourhood gossip, she kept

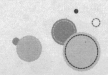

her eyes fixed on her plate. No amount of coaxing or questioning would make her explain what was wrong. She barely ate a mouthful, but just chased the food around her plate with her fork, her chin resting on one hand.

Her parents were really worried about her, and Kim even did the washing up for a mere five dollars to try to cheer her sister up, but Cleo hardly noticed. After dinner she slumped onto the sofa and hugged a cushion to her chest, looking at the TV screen without seeing it at all. Her parents looked at each other and raised their eyebrows. This wasn't like Cleo.

It was a horrible, tense evening. The usual relaxed atmosphere of their house was completely missing, and no one except Cleo knew why. She just sat in the corner of the sofa, trying to take her mind off things by watching TV, but failing utterly.

Finally, when Kim had disappeared up to her bedroom to escape the tension, and their mum had popped over to a friend's house for a

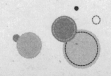

chat, Cleo knew that she wouldn't be able to sleep until she had spoken to her dad. She was just plucking up the courage and trying to find the right words when he got up and went into the kitchen to make a drink. Cleo listened as the kettle boiled and he rattled around with mugs and spoons. They were such familiar sounds, but right now everything seemed weird and unusual.

"Cleo, coffee," he called from the kitchen.

It's now or never, Cleo thought, standing up and walking into the kitchen. Her dad placed two large mugs of steaming coffee on the kitchen counter as she came to sit next to him.

"Dad?" she began, pulling the chair out and choosing her words carefully. "Have you ever caught any sea turtles?"

"What kind of a question is that?" her dad enquired, frowning.

"It's simple," said Cleo, a little irritation creeping into her voice. *Why is he being so defensive?* "Have you ever caught a turtle in

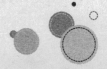

one of your fishing nets?"

"Cleo, you know me," he replied, sipping his coffee. "I do what's right. Okay?"

"That's not an answer," said Cleo.

A cold, sick feeling was rolling around in her stomach. She looked sideways at her dad. He was wearing the same open expression as always, but suddenly she found herself wondering if she could really trust it. It was an awful sensation. She felt hot and almost dizzy.

Don looked at her and realized that she was deadly serious. Whatever was going on in her head, she needed an answer.

"We do everything by the book," he said, putting down his mug of coffee and looking hard at Cleo as he tried to explain himself. "We use nets with grids in them. If a turtle comes in, it's directed to an opening."

Cleo was listening carefully as her dad tried to explain to her exactly how the nets worked. She wanted to feel reassured, but the whole

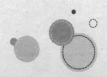

thing just sounded fuzzy and unclear.

"Plus, we fish miles away from the nesting beaches," her dad went on, at a loss as to what else he could tell her.

Cleo just gazed at him and blew on her coffee to cool it down. She didn't seem to have understood a word he said, and she had a very strange, blank look on her face. Don shrugged his shoulders and picked up his coffee again. *Maybe she's using this turtles thing as a conversation opener*, he thought. *I wonder what she really wants to talk about.* It didn't occur to him for a moment that Cleo could be doubting his word.

"Well, some of the turtles are still getting caught," said Cleo eventually.

"Not by me," said her dad firmly, feeling thoroughly sick of this conversation. "And not by any fishermen who's doing the right thing."

He looked at Cleo, wondering what she was thinking. She really did seem hung up on those turtles. *Maybe Bev's right*, he said to himself.

41

Maybe it's just Cleo being a teenager, and I shouldn't worry about it. But he wasn't convinced.

Cleo didn't return his look. She was thinking over everything he had said. Although she had doubts, she had no reason not to trust her dad, and nothing Rikki said was going to change that. *If Dad says he's not catching turtles, then that's the truth*, she thought. *But how am I going to persuade Rikki and Emma? They don't know him like I do!*

Finally, Cleo drained her coffee and went to bed. She lay there in the dark, listening to the waves lapping against the bank outside. It had been a really awful day, and she was glad it was over, but she was dreading seeing Emma and Rikki the next day. *How shall I act around them?* she wondered. *I hate arguments!* She decided to behave as if nothing had happened when she saw them. *After all, I know that my dad hasn't done anything wrong*, she told herself. *It's just going to take a bit longer to prove it to Emma and Rikki, that's all.*

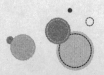

Chapter 6

Bright and early next morning, the sun was glinting off the open water, sparkling as far as the eye could see off the coast. The vast expanse of ocean was broken only by a solitary fishing boat. It was Don Sertori's trawler ... but he wasn't on board. His second in command, Eddie, was the acting captain.

Eddie was a swarthy, tough-looking man with long, greasy hair and a permanent nasty sneer on his face. The crewmen didn't like him one bit, but Don trusted him, and they respected Don, so they put up with Eddie.

Eddie was taking the boat out for Don that day, hoping to catch a massive haul. He wanted the money and the praise that would come with a huge catch, and he didn't really care how he got it. He just had to be fast and lucky. A smirk came over his face as he steered the boat out to

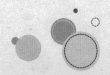

sea. He knew exactly where to go. There was one place where he could guarantee no other fishermen would be, and there would be tons of fish just waiting to be caught. With a low chuckle he set a course for the nesting beaches.

After their adventure on Mako Island, Emma had been forced to give up her dreams of becoming a swimming champion, so she no longer trained officially. But she still woke up early and headed down to the beach – a lifetime habit like that was hard to break. When she woke up in the morning she always craved the feeling of the water around her. She would pull on her bikini and her beach gear, and head down to the shore. The only difference was that now, Rikki was always there waiting for her.

That morning was no different. When Emma arrived at the beach, Rikki was already sitting on a rock, staring out to sea and deep in thought. Her face brightened when she saw

Emma. They usually spent at least an hour in the water, and it was a fantastic way to start the day. Together they jogged into the water and plunged under the waves – just as their legs vanished and were replaced by long, golden tails. They flicked the tips of their tails up in the air as they dived down, and the sun glinted off their golden scales.

Underwater, Rikki and Emma powered through the blue, their mermaid tails flashing past rocks, fish and coral. It was a race! They cut through the water at the speed of torpedoes, trailing bubbles and laughing as they competed to be the best. In delight, they looped the loop under the waves, showing off to each other in sheer joy. When they finally pulled up, they exchanged grins. It was yet another draw!

Emma looked up and suddenly her eyes opened wide. She took Rikki by the arm and pointed. Rikki looked up too, and her face fell. Something dark and vast was blocking the space between them and the surface. A very

large fishing net was swooping down towards them from a trawler above. It ballooned out, scooping up anything in its path … including a small sea turtle!

The girls easily evaded the net, but the poor turtle wasn't so lucky. Emma edged closer to the net, examining it. To her disgust and horror, she realized that it was an illegal one. There were no grids – no carefully placed openings. They watched as the turtle desperately struggled to get free, entangling itself further and further in the strands of the net. It was being dragged along behind the boat, and it would drown long before the net was pulled in.

This is awful, thought Emma. *There must be something we can do to help!* She looked at Rikki questioningly.

The two girls had developed a good understanding of each other's expressions since they had started swimming together. It was impossible to speak underwater, so it was really important to be able to communicate in some

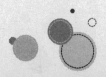

other way. Rikki knew exactly what Emma was asking. They had to do something about the trapped turtle before it was too late – but Emma didn't know how to help. They weren't strong enough to rip holes in the man-made fibre of the net, and they didn't have any tools to help them.

But Rikki had an idea. There was only one place nearby where she would be able to find some tools to help them rescue the turtle. She gave Emma a short, sharp nod and swam rapidly upwards.

On board the fishing boat, Eddie stormed out of the cabin. Jake, his crewman, was standing in the stern, using his fishing knife to cut up some old pieces of rope. His expression was grim. They had been at sea for several hours, and he was already pretty sick of Eddie's attitude.

"Come on, Jake," Eddie yelled. "We won't make quota if we don't move it."

He went back inside the cabin and Jake

scowled at his back. He dropped the rope and put the knife down on the side of the boat. Then he followed Eddie to prepare to haul in the net.

No one saw a hand reaching over the side of the boat.

No one saw the hand grasp the fishing knife and take it.

Rikki gave a wide grin as she disappeared back under the waves, diving down to where the turtle's struggles were growing weaker. *Hurry up!* thought Emma anxiously, as Rikki used the fishing knife to saw at the net. *There isn't much time left!* Emma pulled at the net with feverish speed.

On board the boat, Jake began to pull in the net. The girls clung onto it as they fought to create a hole, using all their strength to hold it back. On the boat, Jake puffed and panted as he hauled the net up. *Must be a good catch today*, he thought.

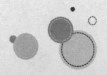

At last the girls managed to open a large, gaping hole – large enough for the sea turtle to swim through. Just in time, the exhausted turtle floated free of the net and paddled away into the blue.

Rikki and Emma watched it swim off and smiled at each other. *At least there's one turtle that won't be hurt by those selfish fishermen!* Rikki thought. She zoomed upwards again and surfaced carefully. Silently, she reached over the side of the boat and replaced the fishing knife. It was then that she recognized the boat. With a flick of her tail she summoned Emma to the surface, and together they stared in horror at Don Sertori's vessel. Before they could say anything, Eddie reappeared and the girls slipped back under the water and out of sight.

It was getting late. Rikki jerked her head in the direction of the coast, and together she and Emma turned tail and raced side by side back to shore. Within seconds they were pulling themselves up onto the rocks. They didn't say

anything – they didn't need to. Each of them was thinking the same thing. How were they going to tell Cleo that her dad was guilty? It just didn't bear thinking about.

Just like Cleo and Emma, Rikki had developed a special power when she became a mermaid. She was able to heat water so fast that it would boil in milliseconds; she had once evaporated an entire swimming pool in three seconds flat. Right now she used her power to dry herself and Emma in double-quick time and restore their legs. Then they grabbed their beach bags and hurried towards the Juice-Net Café, their shoulders slumped and their expressions worried.

On board the fishing boat, Jake had finished hauling in the net. It dangled above them, suspended in the air. Jake and Eddie were staring in horror at the huge, jagged hole in the side. They were in big trouble, and they had a lot of explaining to do. They hadn't caught a

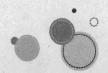

single fish – and something had caused hundreds of dollars' worth of damage to a net without them even noticing. Eddie swallowed nervously and chewed his lip. What was Don going to say?

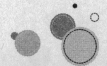

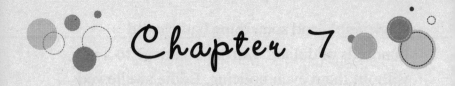

Chapter 7

"Local fishermen today have been confronted with a possible menace from the deep," barked the reporter dramatically. "Commercial fishermen have reported incidents that may involve a rogue shark!"

It was a couple of hours later, and everyone in the Juice-Net Café was silent, listening to the news report that was blaring out of the TV on the wall.

"They were lucky to escape injury, but what could have caused such massive damage to the net?" enquired the reporter, who was milking the story for all it was worth.

Emma and Rikki were sitting together at a table, staring up at the screen. They hadn't said much since they had come out of the water that morning. The beads that hung in the door rattled and they turned their heads as Cleo

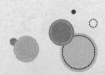

walked in. She saw them and hurried over.

Cleo was eager to make up after the argument they had had yesterday. Now that she had spoken to her dad, she was sure that Rikki was wrong about him. He wasn't like the other fishermen. *I'll find a way to prove it to Rikki*, she thought, smiling at her friends.

"Hey guys," she said. "What's going on?"

She slipped into a chair next to them. Emma and Rikki looked at her with concerned expressions. *How are we supposed to tell her this?* Emma wondered. *I don't even know how to begin!*

Just then there was a shout from behind them. Byron was pointing towards the television screen.

"Hey, Cleo!" he said. "Your dad's on TV!"

All three girls turned to stare at the TV. Don was on the screen, standing in front of his boat and talking to the camera. Eddie and a few other fishermen were standing together talking

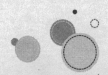

in the background.

"I've fished these waters for a long time," Don said grimly, "and there's only one thing that causes damage like that."

Emma and Rikki looked down, feeling slightly embarrassed.

"A huge rogue shark!" Don continued. There was a gasp from around the café and everyone started chattering.

"Coming up after the break …" continued the newsreader.

The girls turned away from the screen to look at each other.

"Poor Dad!" Cleo cried.

Rikki and Emma exchanged a glance. *I can't do this*, thought Emma. *I just don't know what to say – Cleo's going to be devastated.*

Rikki understood the look on Emma's face. *It's up to me*, she realized. She leaned forward and spoke in a low, gentle voice, quite unlike her usual loud tones.

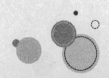

"I'm sorry to have to tell you this, Cleo," said Rikki. "But your dad didn't catch a shark. It was a turtle."

"We cut the net to set it free," Emma added, finding her voice at last.

"No way," said Cleo, shaking her head and frowning. "My dad wouldn't catch turtles."

She glared at Rikki. *This is her doing*, she thought, *It's some kind of horrible trick.*

"It's true, Cleo," said Emma. "I'm sorry."

Rikki nodded. *Poor Cleo*, she thought. *It's terrible to find out that your dad's a liar. How is she going to cope?* She lowered her eyes and bit her lip.

Cleo stared at them. Somehow, despite herself, she could see that they were telling the truth, and it shook her to the core. *If this is true, it means that Dad lied to me,* she thought. *If this is true, how can I ever trust him again?*

She looked down at the surface of the table under her hands. Suddenly, everything seemed

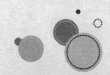

very crisp and clear. The colours and objects around her were brighter and sharper. Cleo knew what she had to do.

Silently, Cleo stood up and left the café. She walked down to the boat wharf and along the line of fishing boats. Fishermen were unloading, doing routine maintenance and tidying their boats, but Cleo didn't notice any of them. Her gaze was fixed on her dad's boat at the end of the boardwalk. She stepped aboard and made her way into the cabin. Her dad was climbing out of the lower cabin as she walked in. She folded her arms and looked at him, half closing her eyes and forcing herself not to cry. Anger, hurt and disbelief were all vying for room in her heart.

"Cleo!" said her dad happily. "I haven't seen you down here for ages! Did you see me on TV? Did I look okay? How about that shark?"

He smiled eagerly at her, imagining that everything was okay between them. Cleo felt as

if there was a huge lump in her throat that she couldn't swallow down. She had always worshipped her dad. Now it felt as if nothing would ever be the same again.

"You don't really know what gets caught in your nets," she stated coldly. "Do you?"

Her dad sighed and the excited gleam went out of his eyes. He examined her face closely and saw how serious she was.

"Is this about that 'turtle' thing again?" he asked slowly.

"Yes," she replied simply.

Tell me it's not true, she was pleading in her mind. *Explain it for me – I'll listen to you! Just tell me how come my friends saw you catch a turtle in your net!*

"Cleo!" her dad exclaimed. "We use the right nets and we fish in the right places."

Cleo's heart dropped. She felt her lips trembling and knew that she couldn't hold the tears in much longer.

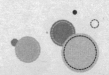

"It's the law, and we do not break it!" Don added.

"I'm really disappointed in you, Dad," said Cleo, her voice cracking as she shook her head in disbelief.

She turned and walked quickly away.

"Cleo!" Don cried, alarmed by her expression.

But Cleo didn't stop. Don watched her go and shook his head. *What has got into that girl lately?* he wondered. *She's not acting like herself at all!*

As Cleo left, she passed Eddie, who was loping towards the boat. As she passed him, he gave her an oily smile, and she hurried away. Eddie walked on board and then paused when he saw Don.

"Oh boss – I didn't know you were back," he said, looking slightly suspicious.

"Well, it's starting to look like I shouldn't go away," said Don.

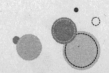

"Sorry we lost half the catch," said Eddie.

"Well, no one can predict a shark attack, Eddie," said Don, trying to be fair about it. "Not even me."

"The net was shredded," said Eddie, feeling under far too much scrutiny for comfort.

It wasn't my fault! he told himself. *Maybe I should have been keeping a closer eye on the sonar scanner, but I couldn't have done anything about a rogue shark!*

He gulped, hoping that Don wouldn't ask him where exactly the boat had been when the net had been shredded. Don was a stickler for the law, and Eddie didn't relish the prospect of admitting that he had been fishing near the nesting beaches.

Don nodded, keeping eye contact with his skipper. *There's something going on here that I don't quite understand*, he thought. *Eddie is definitely looking guilty about something.*

"Where is that net, Eddie?" he asked.

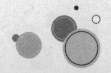

"Well, I dumped it," said Eddie. "What's the point in keeping a wrecked net?"

His forehead prickled with sweat as his boss stared at him. If Don saw that net, he would know that Eddie had been fishing illegally.

Don looked at him for a moment longer, and then nodded. He could sense that Eddie was concealing something, but just then he felt more concerned about Cleo than about the young skipper. Whatever it was, it would keep.

Don walked out of the cabin and Eddie breathed a sigh of relief. With any luck, he was going to get away with it. He chuckled softly to himself. *I can get away with anything*, he thought with delight.

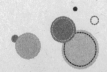

Chapter 8

Cleo raced back to the Juice-Net Café. Rikki and Emma were outside, waiting for her. As soon as they saw her expression, they knew that she finally believed them. They followed her into the café, feeling guilty and miserable. Just because they were right, that didn't mean they felt good about it.

The café was as busy as usual. A couple of kids were playing pool, and more were grouped around a computer. All around them were listening ears, but Cleo didn't care who heard her. All she could think about was the fact that her dad had lied to her.

"He denied everything," she announced. "It's really awful."

They sat down in the only empty seats and looked at each other, feeling helpless.

"I mean, what could I say?" Cleo went on.

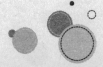

"'I know you're lying, Dad, because my *mermaid* friends saw you fishing close to the nesting beach'?"

She leaned her chin on her hand and groaned. But there were more shocks just about to come.

"He was using illegal nets too," said Rikki, screwing up her face in sympathy, but aware that Cleo needed to hear the whole truth.

Cleo was stunned by this fresh revelation. She turned to Emma as if hoping that she would deny it.

"It's true – and they didn't have those grid things in them," Emma confirmed.

"This gets worse and worse," Cleo whispered in despair. "*My dad!*"

Emma and Rikki exchanged a look. They felt awful about telling Cleo these things, but she had to know everything.

Then Rikki had a thought. There was a tiny chink of hope.

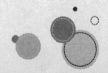

"Well," she said. "To be honest, we didn't actually *see* your dad."

"But it *was* his boat, right?" said Cleo, who would not be comforted.

Emma and Rikki nodded solemnly, and Cleo leaned back in misery. There was no way around it. Her dad was using illegal nets and killing sea turtles, and worse still, he had lied to her about it. *What am I supposed to do now?* she asked herself.

Emma suggested going for a walk, but Cleo shook her head. Right now, she just wanted to be alone. Her world was crumbling around her, and she had to try to pick up the pieces. Reluctantly, Emma and Rikki left her sitting numbly in the café. They all felt as if nothing would ever be the same again.

Emma and Rikki walked towards the wharf, talking in low voices about everything that had happened. Usually there were only a few

people around at that time of day, but right now there were a number of groups heading in the same direction as them, chattering eagerly about the rogue shark.

Down on the boardwalk, fishermen were working hard, sharpening fishing hooks and getting ready to go shark hunting. There were already crowds of people hanging around, watching the preparations. Rikki and Emma strolled through the throng, each wearing a deep frown.

As the girls walked past Eddie, who was sharpening a very, very big hook, Rikki gave a growl of exasperation.

"Great," said Rikki. "Every fisherman on this side of the planet is getting psyched to catch that stupid shark."

"Shark?" repeated Eddie, overhearing them. "Don't you girls worry – if it's still out there, it's going to be sushi."

He held up the hook and leered at them. Emma and Rikki moved away, repulsed. Eddie

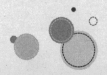

grinned and continued sharpening his hook. Orange sparks spurted from the metal as he brought it to a deadly point.

"What a circus," said Emma, screwing up her nose. "They'll be searching everywhere."

"Want to risk a swim?" Rikki suggested, already knowing what the answer would be.

"No way," said Emma firmly. "It's too dangerous with these guys out there. Let's face it – until this cools down, we're grounded."

Rikki was disappointed, but for once, she agreed with Emma's caution. The last thing she wanted was to see Eddie's hook coming towards her underwater. They strolled past more fishermen and away from the wharf, wondering when they would be able to get into the water again.

Meanwhile, Cleo was leaning against one of the wooden pillars outside the Juice-Net Café, deep in thought. She looked out over the water,

wondering what was happening to her life. *Ever since I became a ... I mean ... I grew a tail, things have been horrible*, she thought. *Everything's been going wrong. I've argued with my friends. I have to pay my sister to do my chores, so I've got no money. And now my dad turns out to be telling the worst lie ever. I don't know what to do any more!*

She stared at the swirling water, somehow soothed by its hypnotic rhythms. All she wanted was for someone to come along and tell her what to do – how to act. But no one was going to do that. She knew that she had to take control of her life before things got completely out of hand. She just had no idea how.

"I know what you're thinking," said a kind, gentle voice.

Cleo looked up to see Lewis standing next to her. She hadn't even heard him approach.

"Rikki and Emma told me about your dad," he went on.

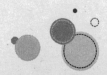

"Great – so now the whole world knows my dad's a criminal," said Cleo, her mouth turning down at the corners.

Lewis closed his eyes for a moment. *I'm not the whole world*, he thought sadly. *I'm your friend, and all I want to do is help you.*

"What would you do, Lewis?" Cleo asked after a pause.

She looked up at him, wondering if he could tell her what to do for the best.

"I'd change my name and move to the country," said Lewis wryly. "But that's just me."

"You're no help," said Cleo sadly, half closing her eyes.

"Oh come on," said Lewis, trying to cheer her up. "At least it takes your mind off the whole … you know … mermaid thing."

Cleo was suddenly hit by a need to talk – to admit what she had been keeping bottled up inside. Her feelings and thoughts about being a mermaid had been kept at bay for a while by

the situation with her dad, but they were still there, and she suddenly had the strongest feeling that everything was linked. She wouldn't be able to sort out the turtle problem until she had come to terms with her mermaid secret.

"Okay," she said slowly. "I'm scared of it – is that what you wanted to hear?"

Why is it always Lewis who ends up hearing this stuff? she wondered. *I guess it must be because he's such a great listener.*

Lewis's head whipped around and he gazed at her, surprised and delighted that she had opened up. She stared back at him, half challenging and half afraid. The expression in his eyes turned from surprise to concern.

"Cleo, *everybody* is scared of something," he said gently. "But *you* – you're amazing – you can do *anything*."

Cleo rolled her eyes. *No one in their right mind would describe me that way*, she thought. *Rikki? Sure thing. Emma? Definitely. But me?*

There's just no way.

"Just because I've got these … powers … doesn't mean I'm amazing," she said eventually.

She gave him a final, sad look and then turned and walked away.

Lewis stayed where he was, staring after her. When she had disappeared from view, he turned his head again and stared out to sea, where the fishing boats were all heading out to hunt for the non-existent rogue shark.

"I didn't mean the powers," he said softly.

He scuffed his shoes against the decking, and then turned and walked back into the café.

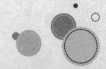

Chapter 9

Cleo walked home slowly and sadly, kicking her shoes against the walls as she passed them. Usually home was a sanctuary for her – a place to escape to whenever she needed it. But right now, home was the very last place she wanted to be. She didn't know how she was going to face her dad, now that she knew the truth.

As soon as she got in, she slipped up to her bedroom and locked the door. Then she ran herself a hot, bubbly bath and sank into it. She counted to ten and watched miserably as her legs vanished and her golden tail appeared.

That's another thing I can't enjoy like I used to, she thought. *Baths used to be such a great way to relax, but now they're just … weird.* She looked down at her tail and flapped it a couple of times. *And I guess I'll never be able to take a shower again.*

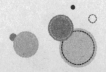

When she had dried herself off and her legs had returned, she drew the curtains and lay down on her bed, her hands flat beside her body and her face expressionless. Usually when she was upset about something, tears came easily. But right now she couldn't cry. She just had a hollow ache in the centre of her body, and she didn't feel like speaking to anyone or making any sort of noise at all.

The sun was setting and dark clouds were scudding across the sky when Don arrived home. He immediately looked for Cleo, who was usually downstairs helping to prepare dinner, but she was nowhere to be seen. It was only when Bev called her for the third time that she appeared and slid into a chair at the dinner table. Don tried to catch her eye, but she wouldn't even glance in his direction.

"Are you going to catch that shark tomorrow, Dad?" asked Kim.

"Maybe," he said. "The council's put out a bounty. Everyone's going to be looking for it. If

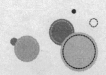

we run into it – we'll pick it up."

Kim gave Don an awed look, and Cleo glanced at her sister jealously. Kim still thought that their dad could do no wrong. Cleo longed to believe that again, but it was too late. She felt as though she were a completely different person from yesterday.

Don carried a large serving platter over to the table. Lying upon it was a huge, whole fish, steaming hot and surrounded by vegetables. Cleo stared at it as her dad placed it on the table. She looked at the scales and thought about her own tail. She thought about the sea turtles that might have died so that this fish could appear on their table. Suddenly her stomach lurched and she knew with absolute certainty that she couldn't eat the fish. It would feel as if she was eating a part of herself.

Cleo's mum picked up the serving spoons and looked across the table at her. Her daughter had gone a very funny colour. Bev had never seen her look so serious or so unhappy.

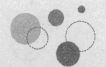

"What's the matter, Cleo?" she asked.

Cleo just shrugged, wishing that she was on the other side of the world. She had no energy left to want to argue. She could barely raise the energy to open her mouth and speak.

"Not hungry," she said.

Everyone stared at her, completely astonished. Cleo usually had a great appetite.

"It's fish!" said her dad in surprise. "Come on – eat."

Cleo glanced towards him and met his eye. Immediately she felt her hackles rise and her voice sharpened. *Who are you to tell me what to do?* she thought. *You've got no right to order me around – not after what you've done.*

"Like I said, I'm not hungry," she repeated. Communicating with her dad had never felt like such an effort before.

Cleo's mum looked at her and raised her eyebrows. *What's wrong with Cleo?* she wondered as she served up the food.

"I caught it this morning," said Don, who was eager to repair his relationship with Cleo – whatever it was that he had done wrong. "Fresh from the *Esmerelda*."

There was a moment's pause as the full meaning of his words sank in. Cleo stared at her dad, his last sentence ringing in her ears.

The Esmerelda, she thought numbly. *He said the* Esmerelda *– didn't he?* She felt as if fireworks should have gone off, or a dramatic piece of music should have been played. What her dad had just said was completely, wonderfully, stupendously momentous.

"The *Esmerelda*?" she repeated at last, hardly daring to believe what she had just heard. "I thought you were in your own boat this morning?"

Her dad shrugged and held out his hands in an expressive gesture.

"If you run three boats you've got to be flexible," he said simply. "Gus is in hospital. I'm

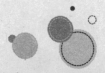

skippering the *Esmerelda* for him 'till he's back on deck."

A wonderful, joyful feeling of relief was cascading through Cleo's body. *If I wasn't sitting down I think my knees would give way*, she thought. Her dad hadn't been lying to her! He hadn't been carelessly killing sea turtles! The world that had been falling apart was magically whole again. A light entered Cleo's eyes as she looked intently at her dad.

"So you weren't on your boat this morning?" she said, wanting to hear him say it again.

"I *just* explained!" said Don, taking his plate from Bev.

He looked at Bev and Kim, who were looking as confused as he felt. He was beginning to wonder if Cleo had received some sort of knock to the head, because she was acting so bizarrely.

A flicker of a smile swept over Cleo's face, and then she frowned again.

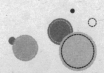

"So you don't really know what it's been catching or where it's been fishing?" she insisted quickly.

"Eddie's skippering for me," said Don. "I trust his judgement. I'm sure he wouldn't do anything wrong."

Everything was falling into place. Behind her dad's back, Eddie was using his boat to break the law. Cleo opened her mouth to reveal the truth, and then closed it again. *How can I possibly tell him what I know?* she thought. *The only proof I have is the word of two mermaids. If I tried to tell Dad that, he'd be on the phone to the doctor!*

Don was staring at her, wondering what this sudden interrogation was in aid of – and when it was going to end. But Cleo didn't have any more questions. She just looked at him and nodded. Don raised his eyebrows, and then looked down at his plate and held it out to his wife.

"Maybe one more," he said, eyeing the

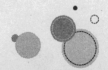

platter of fish and vegetables.

Bev laughed and put another helping onto his highly piled plate. Then everyone began to eat – everyone except Cleo. She couldn't think about food.

She leaned back in her chair, her mind racing. She finally understood what had really been going on … but what on earth could she do about it? *I don't want to tell Emma and Rikki yet,* she thought. *They might just think that Eddie's following my dad's orders. No, first of all I need to get some proof. I need to spy on Eddie and his crew!*

Cleo toyed with the idea of stowing away on board the trawler, but she soon dismissed it. There was nowhere she could hide on her dad's boat. Besides, she didn't really want to be far out at sea with a slimy crook like Eddie. *No*, she decided, *the thing to do is to hide somewhere near the boat and listen to what they say. The minute Eddie gives himself away, I'll tell Dad. Then I'll make sure he's sorry he hurt*

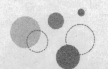
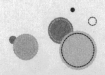

those little turtles!

A little smile lifted the corners of Cleo's mouth and she gazed at her dad, feeling strangely protective over him. *He's the best dad in the world,* she thought. *No one's going to call him a criminal and get away with it!*

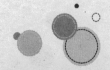

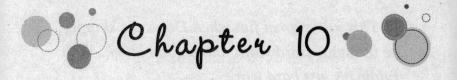

Chapter 10

Early the next morning, Eddie and his crewmen, Jake and Johnno, were getting Don's boat ready to put out to sea. They were late because Eddie had overslept, and now Eddie was racing around the boat, barking orders and blaming everyone except himself – as usual.

"Hurry up!" he snapped out. "I don't want to be the last to leave *again*!"

Maybe you should set your alarm clock better, then, thought Johnno viciously, as he worked at double-quick speed, trying to make up for lost time.

Johnno was an easy-going guy, but he was finding it more and more difficult to ignore Eddie's bad attitude and inept leadership. He was just hoping that Gus would soon be out of hospital so that he could go back to working with Don.

This job is great fun when Don's the skipper, he thought. *Hard work, but a good laugh. With Eddie it's just hard work.*

Unseen by Eddie or Johnno, there was a slight movement on the boardwalk nearby. Behind the wooden supports of the boardwalk, squeezed between old lobster pots, tangled ropes and buoys, Cleo was crouching down and listening to every word. She had arrived early and watched the various crews take their boats out to sea. She knew that fishermen were supposed to start early, and she had almost given up on seeing Eddie when he had finally turned up. It made her furious to think how much her dad trusted this man, and how badly his trust was being repaid.

"We've got to make up for the catch we lost yesterday," Cleo heard Eddie saying, "so we've got a big day ahead of us. Cast off!"

I can't believe that they let him speak to them like that, thought Cleo. She had never once heard her dad treat anyone so rudely.

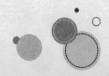

Just ignore him, Johnno was telling himself. *Get on with the job and ignore him. Don'll be back soon enough.*

"We're heading for Patterson's Beach," Eddie told him.

Cleo gasped and put her hand up to her mouth. That was the beach where most sea turtles went to lay their eggs – no one was allowed to fish there!

"Hey, Patterson's Beach is a no-go zone!" said Johnno, pausing and turning to squint at Eddie. He couldn't let something like that pass without an argument.

Cleo nodded vigorously.

"And we're using the old nets too, Johnno," said Eddie in a warning voice. "You got an opinion on that?"

"Yeah," said Johnno, who wasn't intimidated by Eddie's swaggering. "The boss won't want us to do that."

"There's only one boss on this boat,

81

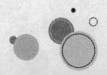

Johnno," Eddie snarled, "and that's me! Just be quiet and do your job."

Cleo drew in her breath sharply when she heard this, and half rose out of her hiding place. The boat backed slowly out of the wharf as Johnno hurried along the deck. It chugged towards the open water, with Eddie standing at the helm.

Cleo slowly emerged from behind the ropes and pots, her eyes fixed on the boat. Her expression was grim as she walked the length of the boardwalk and stopped at the very end. Her breath was coming in short bursts and her heart was thumping. *I have to stop them!* she thought, her mind whirling. *There's no one else to do it!* But she couldn't seem to move a muscle.

As she watched the boat head out to sea, she heard a step on the boardwalk behind her. It was Lewis, and he was carrying his fishing gear.

"Cleo!" he exclaimed. "What are you doing here?"

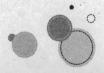

Cleo didn't even turn around. She raised a trembling arm and pointed out to sea at Don's boat, which was getting smaller and smaller as it chugged away from them. She tried to speak, but she was shaking inside, and speech wasn't possible for a moment.

"What's wrong?" Lewis asked.

"They're using the wrong nets and going to the wrong place," said Cleo, finding her voice. The words spilled out of her, and each one seemed to heighten the tension inside her. She felt like a coiled spring.

"Are you okay?" Lewis asked, sensing that she was not her usual self, but not quite sure what the change actually was.

Cleo was undergoing a sort of transformation. She felt as though a part of her that had always been there, but had never been needed, was suddenly coming to life. Her thoughts were suddenly crystal clear and she knew precisely what she was going to do. There was no fear inside her at all at that moment, just an

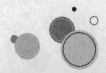

unbreakable determination.

"Yes," she replied, matter-of-factly. "I'm going to stop them. Go and tell the others."

Lewis gaped at her.

"Wh-what?" he said, unused to hearing her give orders.

"Just go!" Cleo yelled in desperation.

Lewis was stunned. He had never heard Cleo sound so ... determined. He turned to obey, but he had only taken a couple of steps when he heard a loud splash. He froze and then wheeled around, half knowing what he was going to find.

Cleo had disappeared. In the water next to the boardwalk there was a small circle of foaming bubbles. As Lewis watched, they grew fainter and fainter until they died away altogether. He knew that somewhere deep underneath the surface was a mermaid who hated the water.

"Cleo?" he said in a squeaky voice.

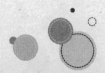

There was no reply.

"Oh great," said Lewis, frantically peering down into the water. He couldn't see a thing. *What am I supposed to do now?* he asked himself in confusion.

There was only one thing for it. He had to find Emma and Rikki – and he had to do it as fast as possible!

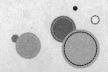

Chapter 11

Help! Help! Help! thought Cleo wildly.

She sank down through the water,
surrounded by bubbles, her head in a whirl. For
a second she couldn't even figure out which
way was up. She waved her arms around in a
panic, trying to claw her way to the surface.
Her tail was a dead weight, dragging her down!
She tried to hold her breath, but her heart was
thumping and bubbles kept escaping from her
mouth. She remembered some of the arm
movements that Emma had taught her once,
but they didn't seem to make any difference.
She was still sinking!

I can't reach the surface! she thought in
terror. *I'm going to drown!*

Her hair swirled around her face, keeping
her from seeing clearly. But then something
wonderful happened. Suddenly she gave a little

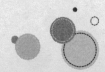

flick of her tail, and she stayed still, hanging motionless in the water. It was as easy as standing up! In astonishment, Cleo stopped flailing her arms around. It didn't make any difference – tiny little movements of her tail were all she needed to keep steady. For the first time Cleo felt connected to her tail – she felt that it was a living part of her, and she knew exactly how to use it. A smile spread slowly across her face as her fears left her. *I was so wrong!* she thought. *No wonder Rikki and Emma thought I was crazy. This isn't scary!*

She looked around. Tropical fish were swimming about. Her long, dark hair drifted in the water. She blinked, looking ahead into the wide, deep blue. There was no turning back now. With a happy sigh she exhaled bubbles from her nose. She was holding her breath, but it seemed like the most natural thing in the world – as natural as breathing air.

Cleo flexed her tail and took off like a bullet, leaving only a trail of bubbles behind her. Swimming was effortless – exhilarating!

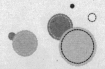

She had never felt like this in the water before! She pulled up and looked around her again, wide eyed. *I did it!* she thought. *I actually did it! I'm in control!*

Don's fishing boat was powering along on the open ocean, close to Patterson's Beach. Eddie came out of the cabin, barking orders at Jake and Johnno.

"Right, no one slacks off today!" he said. "Keep your eyes open for that shark."

Jake and Johnno scowled at him.

"The shark's the least of your problems," said Johnno, as he prepared to unload the net into the sea behind the boat.

"If I get any more lip from you, Johnno, you won't have a job," said Eddie. "Got it?"

Johnno glared at him, but didn't stop unloading the net. Eddie was lazy and arrogant, but he was in charge and the two men had to follow his orders. They knew that Don would be furious if he found out what Eddie was

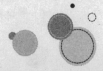

doing, but they were afraid of losing their jobs.

Eddie returned to the cabin, his face screwed up in a scowl. Jake and Johnno looked at each other and shrugged, readying the nets. As the boat chugged along, they released the illegal nets behind them. The nets billowed out in the water, ready to catch anything and everything in their path – including sea turtles.

Not far away, Cleo was coursing through the water with complete ease. She swam slowly over bright corals and past colourful fish, staring in delight at the things she had only heard Emma and Rikki talk about before now.

They're right, she admitted to herself. *This is a wonderland. I've been missing out on the experience of a lifetime!*

Her face glowed with excitement and she was constantly stopping and turning, darting this way and that, trying to take in all the magical sights of the ocean. Briefly, she forgot why she was there in the delight of this new

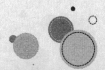

world. Then suddenly, straight ahead of her, she saw a turtle swimming towards a huge, illegal fishing net.

Cleo's heart thumped. She had to save that creature! With a swift gesture she used her powers to send an unstoppable jet of bubbles speeding through the water. The turtle was pushed to one side, missing the net.

Cool, thought Cleo, grinning. *Now I just have to find a way to stop them fishing in these waters!* She was suddenly filled with confidence. If she could do this, she could do anything!

On board Don's boat, Eddie stood at the helm, watching Jake and Johnno at work down on the deck. Then something caught his eye at the side of the boat and he frowned. He leaned out of the cabin door and looked at the shape in the ocean. His brow cleared. It was a sea turtle, breaking the surface of the water to get some air. The turtle almost seemed to be looking right at him.

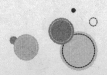

A faint smirk passed over Eddie's face. *If those turtles are stupid enough to get in my way, that's their problem*, he thought. *I'm too busy saving my own skin to worry about saving them!*

He returned to the helm and continued forward without changing course. But Jake and Johnno were both alert, and it wasn't long before Johnno spotted something in the water. He peered over the side of the boat and then raced into the cabin.

"Hey!" he cried to Eddie. "There are turtles out there!"

"Yeah – so?" said Eddie, as if Johnno had said nothing important.

"So you can't fish here," said Johnno, deeply concerned. "It's illegal. Don will have your guts!"

He stood behind Eddie, waiting for orders to pull in the net. But Eddie didn't move. He didn't stop the boat or begin to turn it around.

"Only if he finds out about it," said Eddie eventually, turning his head and trying to stare Johnno down.

Johnno stared back at him. *You are such an idiot*, he thought.

"You're playing a dangerous game, Eddie," he said.

Eddie ignored him and looked up at the sonar screen.

"Hey, look at that!" cried Eddie.

Johnno looked at the screen, where a large blip had suddenly appeared within range. It was close to the boat – and getting closer. Johnno stared at it in concern.

"That's not a turtle," said Eddie, his voice suddenly charged with excitement. "I'm going about."

He turned the wheel and the boat started to swing around.

Underwater, Cleo swam steadily towards the boat, looking out for more turtles. She had no idea that she had been spotted on the screen, and she didn't realize that the net was slowly changing direction.

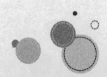

In the cabin, Eddie steadied the wheel and looked at the screen again.

"Looks more like that shark," he said, imagining how great it would be if he caught the rogue creature. "Get ready – I don't want to lose it again!"

Yeah, thought Johnno as he raced out to the deck, *you're just the sort of idiot who would think that catching a rogue shark is exciting!* Johnno looked at Jake, who rolled his eyes. They both knew that it was difficult and dangerous to catch a shark, and they didn't really trust Eddie to know one end of a boat from the other.

This was turning into a really bad day.

Cleo powered along with a flick of her tail. She was entranced by the sight of the open ocean from under the waves. *It's the most beautiful thing I've ever seen*, she thought. Above her, she saw another turtle swimming gracefully along with a couple of fish. Cleo smiled – this was a

million times better than the most wonderful documentary she had ever seen. The ocean was filled with sounds, and the more time she spent in it, the more they seemed to come together like a kind of music.

She was gazing into the endless blue, and she didn't see the huge, billowing net that was flowing up behind her. As it swept up and over her, she turned and began to swim upwards as fast as she could, following the disappearing turtle. But as she shot up, her tail fin got caught in a piece of the net and jerked her to a halt. Her tail twisted and writhed as she tried to escape, but every move trapped her more firmly. Panicking, she clawed at the net, turning around and around. *I can't be trapped like this!* she thought. *I'm more intelligent than a fish or a turtle! I have to be able to work my way out of this!* But everywhere she turned, the blue net was right in front of her, blocking her and pulling her down. She desperately tried to find the opening, but it was no use. She had been well and truly caught!

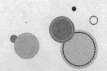

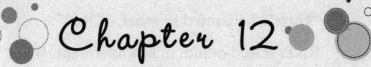

Chapter 12

Lewis raced up to Emma's house from the wharf. He had already searched in the Juice-Net Café and on the beach, but Rikki and Emma hadn't been there. He had no idea where Rikki lived, so Emma's house was his last hope. He burst in without knocking and skidded into the hall, panting and panicking. No one was in the sitting room.

No, no, no! he thought. *They have to be here! Cleo could be in real trouble by now! What if she couldn't work her tail? What if she got seen?* Lewis clutched his head. *I'm babbling,* he thought wildly. *I'm babbling without even speaking! That's got to be a first!*

"Guys!" he hollered.

Then he heard a noise behind him. He spun around and saw Emma and Rikki walking down the stairs. He had found them!

"Guys!" he panted in relief. "Cleo!"

Rikki stared at him in bewilderment. *What now?* she wondered. Lewis had some really great points and he was definitely growing on her, but there was no denying that he could be very weird sometimes.

However, Emma realized that something was very wrong and caught on to his panic. Somewhere, Cleo was in big trouble.

"Well – wh-where is she?" asked Emma urgently.

Lewis could hardly think clearly enough to speak. He pointed downwards, gulping and puffing.

"She's ... she's ... in the water!" he gabbled at last, trying to catch his breath.

"At *last*!" Rikki exclaimed, glancing at Emma. *That's a good thing, right?* she asked herself.

"No!" Lewis stammered, as if he had read her mind. He was pale and his eyes were wide

with fright. "No!"

He shook his head so violently that his bucket hat nearly shot off it.

"Lewis, speak!" Rikki cried in frustration. "Like a normal person!"

What is wrong with him? she thought.

Lewis gave up. There was no way he was going to be able to explain it all and still be in time to help Cleo. *They're just going to have to trust me!* he told himself. He beckoned and raced back out of the door, knowing that Emma and Rikki would follow him. He didn't have time to waste with words. Cleo could be in a lot of danger!

The three of them raced down to the wharf, with Lewis leading the way. He managed to pant out a few words as he ran – enough to get the gist across to Rikki and Emma. Rikki could hardly believe it. She had thought that nothing and no one could persuade Cleo to get into the water, but in the end, all it had taken was a few little sea turtles and an untrustworthy skipper.

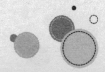

I just hope that she's okay, she thought as they neared the boardwalk. *She shouldn't have gone in alone like that! Why couldn't she have waited for us?*

Lewis flung himself against the boardwalk supports, gasping and red in the face. He pointed at the spot where Cleo had dived in, and Rikki exchanged a glance with Emma.

If anything has happened to Cleo, I'll never forgive myself, Emma thought, her lips starting to tighten.

She looked all around, checking to see if anyone was watching. The crowds that had been there to watch the fishermen preparing to hunt the shark had gone. A few people were working on their boats, but nobody was looking in their direction. She nodded at Rikki.

Without a word, the two girls ran down the boardwalk and dived into the water, disappearing under the waves with two faint splashes. Lewis sank down with his back against the wooden support, wheezing and staring out

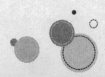

to sea, willing the girls to swim as fast as they could. If they could find Don's boat, they would find Cleo. He just hoped that they would get there before something had happened.

Meanwhile, far out at sea, Cleo had stopped trying to untangle herself from the net. Each time she writhed or twisted, she just made it worse. The net was pressing against her face and she could barely see a thing. She had no idea where the opening of the net might be and there was no way that she could get out. She concentrated instead on holding her breath for as long as she could. She had already been under for ten minutes, and from what Rikki and Emma had said, she knew that she only had another five minutes left. She was scared, but she forced herself not to panic.

There has to be something I can do, she thought. *Surely something will happen to save me. Or I'll think of something.*

She looked all around her, hoping to see

something that she could use as a tool to escape. But all she could see was the criss-crossing blue net, pressing against her body, tail and face, and holding her prisoner as securely as any jail cell.

Things weren't looking good.

Gradually, Don's boat slowed and then stopped. Johnno peered over the stern into the water. He could just make out a large, dark shape in the net. It didn't seem to be moving, but it was definitely not a sea turtle. He raised his eyebrows and raced into the cabin, where Eddie was standing at the wheel.

"Yep, you got it, skipper," said Johnno. "That shark's in the net."

Eddie looked at him with a mixture of triumph and alarm.

"Get it up here before it rips that net to pieces!" he ordered. "It's not getting away from me this time!"

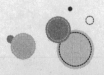

Johnno nodded and raced back out on deck. He pushed the winch lever, and the chains clanked and clanged against the side of the boat as the net was gradually drawn in.

Underwater, Cleo flinched as the net yanked her upwards. *No way!* she thought. *I can't be seen like this – not now I'm finally enjoying being a mermaid!* At first she thrashed about in a panic again, but then she had an idea. She raised her hand and sent a powerful jet of water flowing upwards, pushing her and the net back down. The net stopped rising. *Yes!* she thought. *It's working!*

Eddie grabbed a nasty-looking hook on a pole and joined Johnno and Jake on deck.

"Must be a big one," he said. "It's fighting really hard."

Johnno and Jake exchanged glances. They had seen sharks caught before, and this wasn't

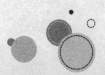

how it was done. *If he thinks he can just destroy a fully grown shark with one blow, he's a mad man*, Johnno thought. *It'll take a lot more than a little hook on a stick to deal with something that size!*

That shark doesn't stand a chance, Eddie told himself, swaggering and posing as the net was reeled in. *As soon as I see it, it's dead meat.*

Cleo was resisting as hard as she could but the winch was still struggling to do its job. She could feel it straining and tugging at her, and, which was worse, she was beginning to feel faint. Her oxygen was almost gone and her chest felt tight and uncomfortable.

Her hand drooped and the force of her power lessened. She was growing weaker. Cleo kept fighting, but her eyes were closing and it was getting more and more difficult to use her power. Her arm drifted loosely to her side and her eyes closed as everything went black.

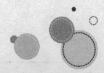

Chapter 13

Just as Cleo was slipping into unconsciousness, two shapes were speeding through the ocean, moving like a pair of torpedoes and leaving a long trail of bubbles in their wake. Emma and Rikki were travelling faster than they had ever done before. They had raced from the wharf at a dizzying speed, rocketing through the water so fast that it made their faces and fingertips start to hurt.

For the first time ever the girls had swum out to sea without noticing the myriad of creatures and plants around them. Lewis had filled them both with a sense of panic, and although they had no idea why, they both felt as if every second counted.

At last they saw the net ahead. It had to belong to Don's boat – there were no other fishermen out in the no-go zone.

Cleo must be around here somewhere, thought Emma desperately. *Lewis was sure that she would follow her dad's boat!*

Rikki was thinking the same thing, but as they drew closer to the net she could see that something was caught inside it. *Not another poor turtle?* she thought angrily. *I'll bet that Cleo's around here somewhere, trying to set it free. These guys really need to be taught a lesson, and we're just the mermaids to do it!*

The girls put on an extra spurt of speed … and then they pulled up sharply and froze in shock and horror. It was no turtle drifting in the cruel net – it was Cleo!

After a split second they darted forward, their arms reaching out to try to help. With trembling, fumbling fingers they tried to free their friend, but she was too twisted up in the net, and the net itself was as strong as steel. Their only chance was to untangle Cleo and then lift her out of the top of the net. But in order to do that, they would have to stop the

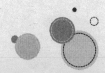

men on board the trawler winching the net up.

Emma shook her head – they didn't have time to mess around or even to worry about being seen. She darted upwards as Rikki kept trying to untangle Cleo from the net. Suddenly she felt calm and in control – she knew exactly what she was going to do.

Emma looked up through the water. She could see the figures of Eddie and Johnno standing in wait at the edge of the boat. The winch was turning fast, mercilessly pulling the net in, and pulling Cleo towards discovery. Emma could see the rope winding back around the winch – rope that had been in the ocean – it was covered in water. She raised her hand and gestured towards the winch. With a grinding, crunching sound, the water on the ropes turned to ice and the net stopped dead. Emma dived down again – there wasn't a second to lose!

On board the boat, Eddie and Johnno looked alarmed as the net stopped feeding back over

the stern. They glanced at each other and then hurried around to the winch.

It must have got jammed, Eddie thought, feeling his heart in his throat. He couldn't afford to lose another of Don's nets – the boss would demand to know where it had happened … and why.

Eddie raced toward the winch … and then stopped in his tracks, staring in absolute amazement. Behind him, Johnno's mouth fell open. The winch, the rope and all the equipment around was covered in a thick layer of solid ice.

Eddie looked up at the blue sky and the blazing sun, and then back at the winch. He cleared his throat and glanced at Johnno, who was looking equally astonished.

Am I dreaming? Eddie wondered. He reached out and gingerly touched the icy winch. It felt cool and glass-like to his fingers. *Why would I dream something like this?* he asked himself. *This is too weird even for a dream!*

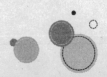

Emma zoomed back down to Rikki. Cleo still wasn't moving, but Rikki had managed to untangle her and find the top of the net. Together they grabbed Cleo and pulled her free of the deadly blue net, shaking as they dragged her up to the surface.

Cleo was a heavy weight as they shot up to the surface, out of sight of the boat. But when they broke the water, Cleo gasped for air.

Rikki let go of her, hugely relieved. *She's okay*, Rikki thought. *She's fine. Now we have to get out of here before those freaks on the boat see us.*

But Emma's heart wouldn't seem to stop thumping. *Any minute now Cleo's going to lose it*, she thought. *Any minute now she's going to realize that she's miles out to sea. She's going to have some sort of panic attack!*

"You okay?" asked Emma, holding on to her friend tightly.

"Yeah!" said Cleo, her voice full of

excitement. "I panicked – I didn't know you could hold your breath for so long. But then I remembered what you guys said. And you know what? I lost count at sixteen and a half minutes!"

She beamed at them, amazed and delighted. Emma smiled too, equally amazed. She had never seen Cleo with this sort of confidence in her own abilities. It was kind of weird – but really great!

Rikki was pleased that Cleo had finally found her fins, but this wasn't the time or the place to start celebrating. It wouldn't be long before the boat turned around and made its way back to shore, and they really didn't want to get in its way. *I've had quite enough to do with boats for one day*, she thought.

"Later guys," she said.

She ducked underwater again and the others followed her. They swam down, twisting and turning towards the beautiful coral reef below. They whooshed past shy clownfish and friendly,

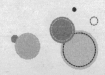

inquisitive yellow tangs. *There's still time enough to show off this awesome place to Cleo,* Rikki said to herself as she pointed out a stunning red fish that she had never even seen before. Cleo let out a sigh of delight and Rikki grinned as bubbles flowed out of her mouth.

I hope that Cleo really is okay, Emma was thinking. *I wouldn't blame her if she never went in the water again!* Then she looked at Cleo and realized that her friend was absolutely entranced. Emma smiled. She and Rikki were now a little more accustomed to the sensations and surprises of the ocean, but she remembered how she had felt the first time she had gone swimming as a mermaid. She and Rikki had played with a young dolphin and explored parts of the ocean that they had never dreamed existed. Now, at last, she would be able to do the same thing with Cleo.

Cleo had totally lost her fear of the water. She could see for herself what amazing times she had been missing out on, and she didn't

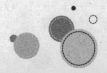

intend to miss any more!

Despite the danger that she had been in, Cleo felt a thrill of excitement as she swam alongside Rikki and Emma at last. She had an overwhelming sense of *rightness* as they moved their tails in unison and smiled at each other. Even her powers felt greater now that she was with the other two – as if they all gave each other strength.

At last Rikki caught Emma's eye and Emma jerked her head towards the shore. They had been out at sea for long enough, and Lewis would be in a state of advanced panic if they didn't return soon. Together, the three mermaids disappeared in a cloud of bubbles as they turbo-swam home.

On the surface, Eddie, Jake and Johnno were still staring in silence and disbelief at the frozen equipment. Eventually, Eddie snapped out of it and starting barking orders. They couldn't move the boat until the net was pulled in, and

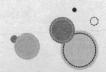

the net couldn't be pulled in while the mechanisms were frozen. Jake and Johnno started boiling water on the little stove in the cabin, while Eddie peered over the stern at the net. Whatever they had caught earlier, it had long since escaped. He scowled and yelled at Jake and Johnno to hurry up. Don would want an explanation why they had caught nothing for a second day running, and Eddie wasn't looking forward to that conversation.

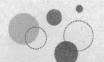
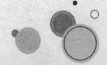

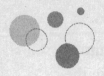 # Chapter 14

The three girls came in to shore on their secluded beach and Rikki quickly dried them off with her powers. As soon as they had their legs, they raced back to the wharf and found Lewis still sitting on the boardwalk, leaning against the wooden supports. He leapt to his feet and gave a huge sigh of relief when he saw Cleo coming towards him.

Rikki and Emma took Lewis for a smoothie in the Juice-Net Café, to calm his nerves and tell him everything that had happened. But Cleo had something to do that couldn't wait. She promised the others that she would catch up with them, and then walked slowly down the boardwalk to where the *Esmerelda* was moored.

Don was coiling ropes on the deck of the *Esmerelda* when he looked up and saw his

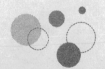
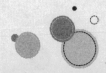

eldest daughter gazing at him.

"Cleo!" he exclaimed in surprise.

He strode across the deck and looked down at her. She was frowning, and he could tell from her expression that this was no casual visit.

"Something wrong?" he asked in concern.

"Dad, I have to tell you something," she said.

Don nodded and put one foot up on the side of the boat, leaning on his knee, ready to listen.

"And I know you're not going to like it." Cleo added.

She began to explain what Eddie had been doing over the past few days. She told her dad all about the illegal nets and the trapped sea turtles. She told him about the conversation she had overheard earlier that day, when she had discovered that Eddie planned to fish in a no-go zone. She told him how Eddie had bullied Johnno and threatened him.

Don's frown deepened as he listened, and

his jaw clenched. As Cleo finished what she was saying, they saw Eddie's boat chugging in to harbour. Cleo looked at her dad's face and swallowed hard. *Dad hardly ever gets angry*, she thought, *but when he does, he's terrifying. I really don't envy Eddie right now.*

Don sent Cleo to catch up with her friends at the Juice-Net Café, and then he finished a few last jobs on the *Esmerelda* as he waited for Eddie's boat to moor.

Eddie raced around the vessel, hastily covering his tracks. He had to make sure that there was no trace of the illegal net or the ice that had spread over half the equipment. It had taken twenty pans of boiling water to loosen the ice, and even now there were still a few shards of it lying about. Not only that, he had to come up with a satisfactory reason why he hadn't caught any fish that day.

Out on the deck, Johnno was working hard, coiling ropes and tidying the boat. His face was

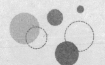
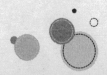

tight and angry. Then his eyes flicked sideways as Don stepped into the boat, unseen by Eddie. Johnno could see from Don's expression that he had somehow found out about what Eddie had been doing. Relief washed over Johnno like a wave.

"You got rid of the net?" Eddie yelled at him through the cabin door.

Johnno didn't reply. Eddie sat down for a rest and a think.

"What net, Eddie?" asked Don, walking in and looking down at him.

Eddie's face went pale and fear leapt into his eyes. Like all bullies, he was a coward, and he didn't have the brains to talk himself out of it.

"Didn't you hear me, Eddie?" asked Don, his voice as hard and cold as iron. "I asked, 'what net?'"

Eddie's lips trembled as Don fixed him with a piercing glare.

"The … um … the net that …" he

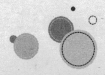

stammered, desperately trying to think of an explanation that would get him off the hook. But his brain just couldn't work that fast. He lapsed into mumbles and then into silence.

There was a long, ominous pause as Don continued to stare at him.

"Johnno?" Don called eventually.

Eddie looked down and hung his head. He knew that he was beaten.

"Yep?" said Johnno, appearing instantly.

"Why don't you tell me what's been happening here."

"Happy to, boss," said Johnno, looking grimly at Eddie.

When evening fell, the Sertori family was again gathered around the dining table, preparing for dinner. But this time, Cleo's mood was completely different. She listened eagerly as her dad told them what had happened with Eddie. Johnno had told him everything, and

there had been a lot more going on behind Don's back than just illegal fishing. Eddie had been slacking off, helping himself to equipment and even breaking quota.

"I fired him," said Don. "I trusted Eddie and he broke every rule in the book. I couldn't keep him on after that."

"You are so tough, Dad," said Kim, as she placed a bowl of peas next to him.

Don gave Kim a half smile. He hated having to fire anyone, but with Eddie he had had no choice. It didn't make him feel very happy though, and that showed in his face. Cleo gave him a sympathetic smile and put the salt and pepper on the table.

"The turtles will thank you for it," she said, trying to cheer him up.

Don looked at her thoughtfully. She had known more than she could have overheard from just one conversation. She had known things that only Eddie and Johnno had known,

such as the exact type of net they had been using. And how had she found out enough to want to eavesdrop on Eddie in the first place?

"How did you know he was using the wrong nets and fishing in the wrong areas?" Don asked his daughter.

"I heard a whisper," said Cleo. "Full of mystery, the sea. Right, Dad?"

"Yeah, sure," he said.

Cleo smiled at him and Don gave her a quizzical look. She had changed somehow – even since that morning. She almost seemed older – more grown up. *And has she grown taller?* he asked himself. *Maybe she's just standing straighter. Whatever it is, something's really boosted her confidence.* A horrible thought suddenly struck him. Had Cleo found herself a boyfriend? *I'm not sure I could cope with that kind of stress after the day I've just had*, he thought.

"I'm sorry for doubting you, Dad," Cleo went on.

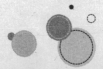

She came to stand next to his chair and leaned down to plant a kiss on his forehead, throwing her arm around his shoulder. Don smiled and hugged her back. Things were back to normal between them.

Just then, Cleo's phone rang. She moved away from the table and took the call. It was Lewis, asking whether she wanted to meet up. He was just dying to know what had happened to Eddie.

"Lewis," she said, with a new confidence in her voice. "Yep, look – tomorrow morning. There's something I want to show you."

She arranged to meet him down on the beach, and then she hung up and went to join her family for dinner. Finding out that she loved being a mermaid was awesome – it was the most exciting thing that had ever happened to her. But finding out that her dad hadn't been lying to her was the best feeling in the whole wide world.

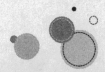

Chapter 15

The next morning was glorious – clear and bright and warm. Cleo jumped out of bed early, pulled on her beach gear and raced over to Emma's house. Rikki was already there, sipping orange juice and regaling Emma with jokes that made her snort with laughter. Cleo waited impatiently for them to get ready. *I can't wait to see Lewis's face!* she thought. *Without his help, I might never have made it out of that net.*

Meanwhile, Lewis was walking towards the part of the beach where Cleo had asked him to meet her. Then he paused and looked down. In a secluded spot, the tops of several turtle eggs were visible, half buried in the sand. Lewis let out a long, amazed breath. He had seen turtle eggs before, but it was always a magical sight.

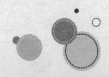

He knelt down next to them and began to gently push sand over them to protect them. Just then, Cleo, Rikki and Emma walked up. They stopped as they saw him on his knees.

"Guys, look!" cried Lewis. "Turtle eggs!"

"Oh!" Cleo exclaimed, crouching down beside the eggs. "Little turtles are so cute. I hope they all make it."

Lewis smiled at her, brushed the sand off his hands and stood up. *That's one of the reasons I like Cleo*, he thought. *She's so kind, and she always sees the magic in stuff like this.*

"So, you wanted to show me something?" he enquired.

"Yes, I do," said Cleo. She looked at Rikki and Emma and her eyes sparkled. "Ready?"

The three girls smiled at one another, pulled off their beach gear and revealed their bikinis. Then they ran into the sea together, laughing. Lewis clambered up onto a rock, turned and then sat down to watch.

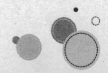

Rikki and Emma were both holding back, their blonde hair floating in the wind. This was Cleo's moment. She was out in front, looking confident and relaxed as she raced into the waves. Lewis had never seen her looking quite so beautiful.

The three girls dived into the water …

… and then three tails rose up in perfect timing and disappeared under the foaming waves. At last the friends were all out there together, exploring the ocean and discovering countless wonders and treasures. Lewis watched, squinting as he gazed out at the horizon. Then he saw a single arm rise out of the water and wave at him. A huge smile spread over his face.

"Cool," he said.